Gray Goose Down

Billy Martin

authorHOUSE®

AuthorHouse™
1663 Liberty Drive
Bloomington, IN 47403
www.authorhouse.com
Phone: 1 (800) 839-8640

Published by AuthorHouse 08/17/2017

ISBN: 978-1-5462-0456-5 (sc)
ISBN: 978-1-5462-0455-8 (e)

Print information available on the last page.

This book is printed on acid-free paper.

Is there someone watching us? What would happen if the two worlds met for the first time?

Is there life be on our own? Have we been visited by those of another World? The event that takes place in this story is a possibility. It provides us with what could happen in the event that two Worlds meet for the first time.

The USS Enterprise is one of the Navy's first nuclear powered aircraft carriers, nicknamed "The Big E," it carries on its deck the Phantom F-4 Fighter jet.

Lieutenant Daniel Gray and Red Hansen are preparing the Gray Goose for its last flight after years of combat duty. The Gray Goose is to be retired as one of the Navy's most decorated combat fighter jet. Unexpectedly, one of the most unusual events occurs during a test flight which changes the course of history for the Gray Goose, and a confrontation that could change the course of history of what we really know.

Chapter One

The Enterprise cut through the blue water with ease as I was making its way back to port after four months of navel drills. Everyone aboard was eager for their time for leave including Lt .Daniel Gray and his engineer Red. It would be a special day for the Gray Goose as it had made its last military run and would be retired having achieved great combat victories. But one last fight would be made to test new advances in aviation using the Gray Goose.

Captain Edington announced that the test would be taking place at 0900 and would last only 1 hour. "Please prepare the Gray Goose." He then called Lt. Gray and flight engineer Red to the flight room.

"Gentlemen, before we can put into dock we have to complete this test flight. And it is my understanding that the Gray Goose has the honors of performing this flight." Edington stated as he pulled down a map from the ceiling." I want you to pay special attention to these island that have been marked in red. Your flight can go anywhere but near these islands. They belong to a drug lord and are off limits to any US military branch. The ATM and Narcotics Department are handling any and all issues pertaining to these Islands and their activities. So with that all said. You flight needs to stay to the East of this area. Now I was told that this should take about an hour to complete. Is that right Red? He asked.

"Yes sir, No more that 50 to 60 minutes to gather all the information. The flight recorder will record all the data gathered. All we got to do is get the Gray Goose up there, the computer will perform the maneuvers." Red replied back as he was reading from the instructions he was given.

"Okay, let's get this done so we can get out of here and get home."

Gray and Red saluted Edington and made their way out of the flight room to the deck. The Gray Goose had already been prepped and was ready. The F-4's newly painted gray color and red markings made her stand out above the rest. The Gray Goose was a proud fighter and Lt. Gray was proud to be it pilot. He was even more excited that this would be its last flight. The Gray Goose would be on display for the public to see, the most honored and decorated F-4 fighter jet in the Navy. A new paint job with new red trimming with brightly placed decals would bring her great honors and be retired with grace.

"Lt., the Gray Goose is ready and willing. We just need someone to point it in the right direction." Red proudly said,

"Let's get this done Red. I've got a dozen letters to write and I want to call home before it gets too late." Lt. Gray said as he completed the last adjustments of his flight suit. "I'll meet you on the fight deck." He replied to Red who was still making some adjustments.

Red had been Lt. Gray's flight engineer since the two had been assigned to the Enterprise. Red was the best there was and Lt. Gray didn't trust anyone else with the Gray Goose. Red knew every nut and bolt that went into the making of the Gray Goose.

Red finally reached the flight deck and climbed the ladder and got himself into seat.

"So this is it Red? Peterson said as he helped get Red locked into place. Adjusting the straps that held Red in place.

"Yep, this is it. One last flight and that the end of The Gray Goose flight days." Red said.

"What a history this bird has got. More than any other one on deck," Peterson replied. "Okay your set. Try not to fall out of this bird okay."

"Don't worry, besides if I do, you're not the one who will come after me." Red said. "Okay, get out of the way your blocking my view. Lt., lets crank this baby up and get this done."

"Roger," Lt. Gray replied as he prepared the Gray Goose completing the last of his check list. The canopy closed and they waited.

They finally got the signal they needed and the Gray Goose propelled itself off the deck of the Enterprise. Everyone watched as the Gray Goose spread its wings and made its way to the East. Its flames were bright, and powerful. She sliced through the air with ease.

"Are we good? Gray asked Red.

"We are good." Red replied. "We're always good. I'm good, you're good."

"I took Peterson up once so he could see what it was like. He got so sick soon as we took off. He never wanted to go again."

"He's better off with his feet on the ground anyway," Red replied. "Some people are born to fly and others, well, they need to stay on the ground."

"What is this flight all about anyway? They made so secret at first, they didn't want anyone to know anything about it," Gray asked.

"I can tell you this now. The Gray Goose has be retrofitted with a computer that instructs her in simulated combat maneuvers. It's for the next generation fighter jets. At least that what they told me. It's going to tell them how they can achieve better agility and better close range dog fight capability. Stuff like that."

"So what do I do? Gray asked.

"Just get us up into the air, and the computer will take over and you just sit back and enjoy the view." Red replied.

"That's it?

"That's it." Red replied. "Technology, isn't it great. Let me tell you this, someday there won't be a need for a pilot. The pilots will be sitting in some nice stuffed chair, with a soda and a sandwich next to them, and a control panel in front of them directing their fighter planes."

Chapter Two

"Red you just about ready to start? Lt. Gray asked as he'd been circling for several minutes waiting for some direction.

"Roger" he replied. "Give me a minute to hit the start button and get this computer program downloaded. It's going to tell us what maneuvers it wants, then it will do it.

"Well, hit the button twice, let's go."

"Enterprise this is the Gray Goose. Where ready to start the run. Are your eyes on us? Red asked.

"Gray Goose, this is the Enterprise we have you locked in and you are given the go."

"Finally," Lt. Gray stated. "Let's crank this lady up."

"The computer is on and now in control." Red replied.

The Gray Goose began executing maneuvers that were designed and executed by the computer program. It made several evasive maneuvers, descended and then climbed with ease.

"Are you sitting back Lt. enjoying the view? Red asked.

"That's a Roger." The Lt. replied. "These turns are sharp. Sharper than I've ever experienced. Even in combat I never executed a maneuver like that. That would take some getting used to. I'm surprised this lady has it in her to do this.

"Roger on that. Red replied. "This old gal still has it in her, even as old as she is."

"Enterprise how are we doing, you able to follow us?

"Roger Gray Goose. You're the only dot in the sky"

"Behave yourself, Captain Edington is coming this way."

"Roger Enterprise."

Captain Edington walked over to the control panel and watched green screen. He knew something about flying but not these types of F-4 fighter jets. Thirty years in the Navy, he was just about to retire and begin a life as a civilian, one who wonders from one golf course to another.

"Where are we," He asked

"Were just about finished sir. Maybe fifteen minutes left with the program and we can bring the Goose home.

"Alright. Let me talk to these guys. Gentlemen I know that technology has greatly increased our ability to do many things, ands sense you're doing nothing while the Goose is doing all the work, so buts what's with all the chatter. Let's get this done. You see, my son is coming home from college and I would like to get home before he does, before he cleans out the refrigerator and then takes my car, which I probably will never see again."

"Roger Captain." Lt. Gray replied.

"Sir, Captain Edington."

"What is it?" Edington replied

"I've got something on the screen."

"What is it?"

"Not sure Sir. I not familiar with this, whatever it is."

"What do you mean? The Navy sent you to school didn't they?

"Yes Sir, but this object is totally unknown to me. And it's traveling at such a high rate of speed. Faster than anything I've ever seen. It's hard to stay fixed on it."

"Which direction? Edington asked as he walked over to the radar green screen.

"Well Sir, the computer has it coming from………" there was a hesitation.

"From where sailor? Where did it come from?

"From a North East direction slightly upward direction I believe."

"What do you mean upward direction? Edington asked.

"Upward Sir, like from outer space."

"What, outer space. Is it a rock, or an old satellite?

"No Sir, definitely not a satellite. It would have burned up in our atmosphere by now."

"Then it must be a rock." Edington replied.

"Well Sir, I just don't know, it has the features of some kind of form. I just can't be sure what it is."

"Contact the Gray Goose and tell them to be on the lookout for whatever that is."

"Aye Sir. Gray Goose, this is the Enterprise"

"Go ahead Enterprise."

"Gray Goose we have on screen an object traveling at high rate of speed in your air space. Be aware that you are still bring controlled by the computer simulator system and have only nine minutes remaining.

"Roger Enterprise, We will be watching. Which direction"

"Gray Goose, it is coming from, well sir,"

"Repeat which direction Enterprise?

"Gray Goose, the object is coming from the North East Upward direction."

"Enterprise, explain upward?

"Gray Goose this is the Enterprise, it appears to have come from outer space."

"Enterprise, repeat that transmission."

"Gray Goose, the object is coming in from a North East upward location, they call it outer space."

"Did he say outer space? Red asked as he looked around trying to see if he could see any bright light in the sky.

"He did." Lt Gray replied.

"Must be a rock or something." Red replied back. "Maybe a piece of junk that's been floating around in space for a while. But that can't explain this. Objects like that would burn up in the Earth's atmosphere before ever getting seen,"

CHAPTER THREE

Edington continue to monitor what was going on, but there was some concern about the object location and direction it was traveling. "Run a check on it again."

"Captain Sir, its speed is faster than the computer can handle, I can no longer plot it course. And the Gray Goose is in the same air space."

"Alright have Lt. Gray terminate the program and return."

"Yes Sir. Gray Goose, this is the Enterprise. You have been ordered to terminate and to return immediately."

"This is Gray Goose. We are terminating the program and will return." Lt. Gray stated. "Okay Red, you heard what they said, shut it down and let's go home. I was tired of doing nothing anyway. Shut it down and let's get back to the Enterprise."

"I'm shutting it down," Red replied as he began the process. Over and over he went through the procedure and got no reaction. "Lt, we have a problem, I can't shut it down. It appears to be locked up and doesn't respond to any of the commands. It wants to stay in control."

"Gray Goose this is the Enterprise, confirm that the program has been terminated. It indicates here that you are still executing the programs simulation."

"Enterprise, it appears the computer will not shut down. I have no control of the Gray Goose. We will continue to terminate."

"Captain Edington, the Gray Goose and this object are now on a Collison course."

"What, how long before ……."

"They have maybe minutes now. Its speed is unbelievable and the computer cannot track its data fast enough."

"Gray Goose this is Captain Edington, you have to get out of there, it's coming right at you unless to change directions, eject if you have to."

Red again and again tried to disengage the computer program. He looked around and saw the bright light above them.

"It's no good," Red shouted out, "I not able to shut it down."

"There it is," Gray shouted back, "Brace yourself."

The object, a fiery ball, hurled itself to earth at incredible speed. With the Gray Goose blocking it way. As it came closer, the light was so bright that both had to look away. Suddenly Gray and Red felt the Gray Goose jerk with incredible force and tilt to one side as the object just clipped the Gray Goose's right wing and then continue in a downward direction. The Gray Goose tumbled downward out of control.

"Red eject, eject now." Gray shouted. "Eject now."

The canopy blew off as both Gray and Red ejected from the Gray Goose. They glided through the air tumbling over and over until their shoots finally opened. Hanging in the air, they both watched as a part of military history fell into the ocean never to be seen again. The dark smoke from the object filled the air as the wind carried them Westerly toward the island. The island they were to stay away from. As they watched the island came closer and closer.

The current took them over the small beach area, and above the forest. They could see the camps that were located just off to their left. But saw no one on the ground. Red gave a thumbs up, as Gray did the same. They were both uninjured so far. But where to land became there next objective.

The island was mostly volcanic rock and dense forest. Finding a landing area was going to be difficult. They could stay up only as long as the parachute could hold the air and keep them up. Knowing that the warm air was going to do its work, they were slowly dropping downward. Gray spotted a small section of open area and pointed to Red. They both maneuvered their shoots directing it to the only open space they could see.

Downward the shoots came. Gray missed the mark by only a few feet. Landing in some small rocky area. Red hit the tree line and got hung up into the branches. The weight of the seat was more than what the branch could handle and it suddenly cracked and broke away from the tree with Red landed on the ground below. Red laid still for several minutes. He was not injured, but needed to catch his thoughts. He removed his straps, helmet, and began to gather up the shoot. Para-shoots are like a big white markers and can be seen from a long distance away. He checked his suit and the gear that all pilots carry in case of such an event. He looked around for Lt. Gray and saw him as he was gathered up his shoot and then hid it in the rocks. They both waved to one another and hurried toward each other.

"Are you alright," Gray asked.

"Other than landing in the trees and falling about ten feet to the ground, yeah, I'm okay." Red replied as he sat down on a small bed of lava rocks. "The Goose went down about a mile out."

Gray sat down next to Red. "I know" He said. "Did you see what hit us?

Red stood up looking around. "No, it was just a ball of fire. The light was so bright I had to look away."

"Well, we better get out of sight. I didn't see anyone on the ground so I don't know if they know were here. We need to get to higher ground and make contact with the Enterprise. We need to stay hidden so let's stay along the tree line and get to that area of rocks."

They began their walk staying hidden from sight. Clinging to the edge of the tree line, they hiked for several hours. They came across a dirt road and began to climb upwards through the lava bed until they reached the larger boulders and could see further.

"Let's stop here and rest." Gray said as he took out his radio and turned it on. There's a risk in using the radio. They could be listening and locate where we are. But we have to take that risk. The Enterprise needs to know that we're alive. So I'll use it then turn it off. If I remember the procedure is to use it every hour or two hours and then turn it off and quickly move to a new location."

"This is a very small island, it's not going to take a lot of time to find someone, if you know the island at all." Red commented.

"I know, that's why we need to stay close by the tree line so we can at least have a chance." Gray replied. "The Enterprise will track us."

CHAPTER FOUR

Captain Edington was on the phone calling and providing information concerning the events that took place. He slammed the phone down and turned around in dismay.

"We can't do anything until we hear from Washington," He said as he slammed his fist down. He walked over to a large map that was on the wall. "I want two rescue helicopters ready and on the flight deck in thirty minutes. Have a crew ready and standing by."

"Sir, I have a transmission from Lt. Gray."

"Put it on speaker," Edington shouted out.

"Gray are you both alright? He asked

"Yes sir, we're both alright. I'm going to limit radio time." Gray said. "Contact you in one hour. Gray out."

"He's limiting his time on the radio in case their tracking him. He'll change location after each transmission. I sure hope Washington gives us some direction soon. That's a small island with unfriendly inhabitants. They'll shoot first and ask questions later. Let me know when those choppers and crew are ready."

"We needs to continue to move each time we use the radio. If there tracking us we need to be in a different location should they come looking for us? And they will at some time." Gray remarked. "See those mountain tops just off to our left? Let's try to get there before it gets too dark."

Gray and Red began climbing through the lava bed. It was difficult because the rocks surface is rough and one can easily get cut. They took it slow and steady. Stopping from time to time to rest. It took them several hours to reach the top. They found an area that was hidden away, and gave them some cover.

"I remember when we went through the survival training for this kind of event. But I never thought I'd ever have to use it." Red said as he reached for his small water bottle. I didn't even think about what's in this flight suits. Peterson always handles all the details of flight preparation."

"Yeah, I know what you mean." I never thought we'd ever have to eject. And I hated to see the Gray Goose go down the way it did." Gray stated as he looked around. "But we need to stay alive and not do anything that will get us injured or killed. We need to use what we've learned, and we'll get out of this in one piece."

Taking out his small binoculars, he looks at the surrounding terrain. There's a spot over that ridge. I think there's a clearing below it from what I can see. There are some large rocks. It's not very big but it's large enough for a rescue chopper to land. That could be a good LZ. Let's move just in case they come for us sooner than later."

Gray and Red maneuvered through the rocks to the tree line wanting to remain out of sight just in case someone came by, they could duck into the dense forest area and not be discovered.

"What do you think their doing? Red asked.

"Who?

"On the Enterprise?

"There probably waiting to hear from Washington or the Naval Control and Command. Whoever makes these kind of decisions? They'll talk about it, argue for a while, drink some coffee, argue some more. The Captain probably has several rescue choppers and crew ready to go, but won't do anything until he gets the okay."

"Politics, what a business." Red replied. "My uncle was in politics back home."

"Is that right, where did he go to school to learn that skills?"

"He didn't, he was a used car salesman for fifteen years. I guess that helped him. He used to say if he can sell you a car that had no engine, he's a prime candidate for Politics."

They reached the outer limits of the clearing and moved up into the rocks. This was a good advantage point. One could see a dirt road that led into the forest toward the ocean. And the rocks were large and had areas one could stay hidden in. They rested and waited until the hour came to call the Enterprise. Gray took out the radio, extended the antenna and made his call.

"Gray Goose to Enterprise. Any progress yet?

"No. Continue to follow protocol, talk to you in AM unless we receive info. Understood?

"Understood, Gray Goose out"

Night came quickly and the darkness of the forest made it difficult to see anything. They sat quietly through the hours. There were sounds but nothing that caught their attention. Nothing they needed to worry about ……until now.

"What was that? Red asked.

"What was that sound? It sounded like someone talking. I can't make out what was said. It was kind of grabbled."

"I didn't hear anything. Maybe you need to get some sleep. I'll take the first watch." Gray said as he watched Red continuing to look around. You sure you heard something?

"There it is again, did you hear that? Red asked.

"No, I didn't hear anything." Gray replied back.

Then suddenly Red raised his head up. "You surely heard that."

"I did. I heard that." Gray got up and looked over the rock they were behind. "I don't see anything he whispered. Let me move further over behind those lava rocks."

They both moved quietly and slowly. If someone was there they didn't want to expose their location. The sounds was getting louder and several sounds that were loader, like someone was shouting. Red took out his binoculars and started to scan the area.

"There, look there," Red said. "What is that?" He said with a surprising voice, "I can't make out who there are."

"I don't recognize who or what they are." Gray replied back. He took out his binoculars. "It's too dark to see through these things. Let's get a little closer, remember no noise."

They moved closer continually staying behind the rocks. Both Gray and Red crouched behind some rocks that were above the objects they were looking at.

"What is that? Red said. "My. Look at the size of them. They got to be seven foot tall. All of them. What is that there wearing?

"Quiet Red." Gray replied. "You'll give away our position."

"See the craft over there? I think there working on it. They have some of the panels off the side." Gray remarked again.

"There's smoke coming out of the side of it." Red stated as he strained to see through the small binoculars.

He leaned back against the rocks. "Red, you know what that is? Red looked bewildered. "I'm afraid to ask, what."

"I bet that's the object that hit us. It's being repaired by whoever these being are."

"Beings, did you say being? Are you saying these… are aliens?

"Do you know of any country that has a craft like that with soldiers the size of these are? Look at their head gear. It covers their entire head and has some type of hose going to a small attachment, where you breathe." "You know that Lt. Pete Jenkins volunteered to use his plane, Molly Bee, for the test. We should have let him do it. So what do we do? Red asked.

"I don't know, you're the engineer. You got the creative mind."

"This is not what I studied in school. Engineering says nothing about this. You're the pilot, you make hard split second decisions, what would you do?

"I have no idea. I was hoping you had something in mind." Gray hesitated, "because, because, there's two of them behind us." Gray remarked, as his voice got louder. Red quickly turned and became like a statues. Their eyes were locked on the two beings. No one moved and no one say a word.

CHAPTER FIVE

Both Red and Lt. Gray leaned back against the rocks as directed. Still nothing was said. The two large being stared at them, and they stared back. They stood close to seven feet tall. The skin was an olive green color and very smooth. What little they were able to see. They wore some kind of suit with a variety of electronics attached to their arms and chest. They were heavily padded and protected from the elements. Their heads were surrounded by some type of thin black helmet that allow you only to see their eyes which were dark. A guard surrounded there lower face, nose and mouth with a flexible tube that went around to their back. Possibly some type of breathing tube. It was connected to a canister which was mounted on their back.

The weapons they carried were be on belief. They appeared to be heavy with a short barrel with a variety of blinking lights and unknown objects. Shells of some type... A blade was attached to the end of the barrel, a very sharp blade. Whatever they were, these being meant business. Real business.

"My name is Lt. Daniel Gray and this is my flight engineer Red."

> The two beings looked at one another after Lt. Gray spoke. Still nothing was said between the two.

"We were forced to eject from our jet when an object collide with our air craft. Was that your air craft that hit ours?

Suddenly one spoke. His voice was deep and hard. It crackled and was unrecognizable in sound or words. It sounded like it was coming from a stereo speaker. A language neither had ever heard before. One began to gesture with the movement of his weapon, which needed no explanation.

He wanted them to move and he was directing them which way to go. Gray and Red did just as they were directed to do.

They moved from behind the rocks out into the open area which was located behind a larger pile of lava boulders. A small fire was now burning with two more of the same beings sitting around it. It was not that cold to Lt. Gray or Red, but to them it was probably cold. Both jumped up when they saw Gray and Red appear. They began speaking to one another. One quickly ran off to their air craft, and went inside. Gray and Red were continually directed to keep their backs against the surface of the rocks.

Within a few minutes several others came out and were walking their way. One was strictly of higher rank. The decals on his suit was different than the others and he appeared to be older in appearance. He walked a little slower and had a slight limp. He stood in front of them and examined them from top to bottom. When he spoke the others responded. Then he spoke to Gray and Red.

"What did he say Lt.?

"I have no idea"

He spoke again. His voice was a little louder this time. He turned and said something to those behind him. One left and entered the craft. He returned moments later carrying several objects. One was handed to each individual. They attached them to their suits and made several adjustments by pushing buttons on the units. You could hear faint voices coming out of the units.

"It sounds like their changing channels. The sounds change each time they push one of the buttons." Red said as he watched the being next to him working on the unit. His large hands were accurate as he quickly pushed certain buttons and then listened.

Then suddenly there was a sound that they recognized. One stopped and said something to the one in charge and they all adjusted the units till the sound that they heard was the voice of a word in the English language.

"Did you hear that? That's our language. They have some type of device that has different languages. It probably interprets what is being said and puts into their language, whatever that is." Red explained.

The older one finally got his adjusted and turned to Gray and Red. He began to speak. It took a second before the words came out in English.

"My name is Captain Org. This is our craft. It has been damaged in several areas. Who are you? Why are you here?

Lt. Gray looked at Red. They said nothing at first. Red turned to Lt. Gray. "I think he's talking to you."

"If we are captured by the enemy we are supposed to give them rank and serial number only. Are they the enemy? Does that apply here? Red asked.

"I think the position that were in and the advanced technology kind of has us in a spot." Gray replied.

"Speak slowly so that our units can interpret what you are saying." The Captain of the alien craft instructed. He waited for one of the two to speak, first looking at Red, then Lt. Gray.

"My name is Lt. Daniel Gray and this is my engineer Red. We are from the naval carrier, Enterprise." Gray replied in a slow sentence, pronouncing each word carefully and slowly.

The being next to Captain Org began to get excited at what Gray had said. They continued to speak to one another with some kind of excitement. Then the Captain again spoke.

"Did you say you were from the ship, Enterprise?

"Yes, the USS Enterprise." Gray answered back.

They began talking amongst themselves again with the Captain doing most of the leading. They stopped and again the Captain turned and spoke.

"My men want to know if your Captain is a man called Kirk.

"What" Gray replied? "What's he talking about? Who's Kirk?

There was silence for a few seconds. Red then turned to Lt. Gray.

"Of course, you know Kirk, of the Enterprise."

"What. No, I don't know a man named Kirk."

"You know the TV series about the Enterprise, Captain James T Kirk, Spock, outer space adventures. I have a box of Star Trek books and videos. I'm a treky." Red replied.

"Are you kidding me, there referring to the movie Star Trek? Gray asked.

"That's the one." Red replied. "Look at the big guy how excited he is. They think we are with the same Enterprise."

"Captain our air craft was hit by an object from space. The collision caused us to eject and we landed on this island. Our plane was damaged and lost in the ocean. Was it your craft that collided with ours?"

Captain Org turned and spoke to his men. They talked amongst themselves for several seconds. The leader spoke and the others lowered their weapons. Two of the others turned and left. Only the Captain and one other remained.

"Our craft developed some mechanical failures and we were forced to enter your atmosphere and find a place to make some repairs. It was unfortunate that the collision occurred, but we had little control over our guidance system. We had just enough control to land. Where you injured?

"There was no injuries except for the loss of our plane." Gray replied back.

"I must ask you this, for it is important not only for us but for your world as well. Were we visible to your tracking systems?

"All they were able to see was probably a ball of fire falling from space, that which will probably be explained as a possible meteorite which we have from time to time. The major concern right now is this island were both on? This island is under the control of some very bad individuals that are connected to no country. Once they find out that someone has invaded there island they will come looking for both of us. And finding you here will really become a problem. A major World problem."

"Then we must make our repairs and leave quickly before any of that occurs." The Captain said as he looked over at his craft.

Gray and Red looked at one another.

"What do you want to do? Red asked. "You got that look in your eye. You're cooking something up."

"Captain, Red is my engineer. He's like a repair man. Let us help you and see if we can get you out of here before the entire World finds out about your existence."

"A repair man. Is that what I am?" Red asked.

"We need to make things simple. You're the best at what you do, so go do it." Gray said, then smiled. Gesturing with his head.

The Captain nodded. Red took a deep breathe, then walked slowly to the alien craft. The larger alien followed Red as they walked into the alien craft. The Captain motioned to Lt. Gray to follow him. A fire had been started for warmth. They both sat near the fire. Lt. Gray watched very carefully. Trust of each other was something that both had on their minds. The more they talked, the more they became comfortable with each other.

"You must have many questions Lt." He asked.

"I do Captain, but there are more pressing issues that need attention right now." Gray replied back.

"You are not afraid at what you see?

"This is not our everyday experience Captain Org. We are trained to follow certain procedures, react in certain ways, but this is not something that is in our military handbook."

"When I first saw you, I think I went numb. I didn't know what to think. Not understanding the unknown can be a little scary at first." Gray said.

"But now you feel different? The Captain asked.

"Well, I don't think you're our enemy Captain. You would have done away with us long ago. But I don't think our worlds are ready for this. Seeing you would bring about major problems. Our world would have so many different opinions on what to do, what your purpose is. Just the difference in our appearance would cause great confusion and panic."

"Yes, I agree with you. But the events that brought us here were out of our control. We have been traveling through space for hundreds of your years. Your planet has been visited by us before, in fact, many times. We have always been very careful on our travels and where we go. There are minerals on your planet that can help our planets existence. Some day we may be able to help each other."

"I believe we can Sir and I will do what I can to help as well." Gray replied.

"That is good."

Suddenly Red appeared from the craft. He was somewhat excited that Lt. Gray could barely understand what he was saying.

"You can't believe what I've seen. The force, t3he power that drives this craft is be on anything I've ever seen. The magnitude of the engine is be on any engineering design we could even think of. But I know what is needed to make the fix." Red said as he took a deep breath.

"What"

"A four inch piece of rubber hose and two clamps."

"What, that's it?

"Yep, this repairman has made his evaluation of the problem and I, and the others agree, we can make the fix easily and quickly. They can be out of here in just 30 minutes if we can find some hose." Red said as he stood there like a shining star.

"Are you sure that's the fix? Gray asked.

Red smiled and nodded. "Yep, that's it."

"Did you hear that Captain?

"I did, but where do we find such parts to make this repair?

"Tell him Red, it was your discovery," Gray demanded.

"It's very simple, we find a piece of hose somewhere on this island. Maybe on one of the vehicles in the camp that we saw when we flew over the island. Look, here's what I know. The engine is cooled just like other engines. They use a fluid similar to the coolant we use to cool our car engines. In their case the connecting hose cracked and the fluid leaked out and there engine over heated. But again in their case, things got really out of control. Their guidance system, which is somehow interconnected. There is no damage to their engine, but they're not going anywhere with it the fix. And the thing about it is, it only take about five gallons of fluid to do it. Radiator fluid should do it."

"That's it? Gray asked.

"That's it." Red replied back.

"Captain, do you have any parts?

"No, we have a support craft that is usually available to help but they are two days away."

"That would be too late I'm afraid." Gray replied as he turned to Red. "Well, what are you going to do about this?

"Me." Red said in surprise. "Don't you have a plan?"

"I've got a plan. But I'll need your help captain. And we need to do this tonight."

"What help can I give you? Org asked.

"I'll need one of your men to go with us. When it's fully dark we are going to slip into the camp that we saw and find the materials that are needed to make the repairs. They was a large building with several trucks and smaller vehicles. They must have a garage as well to take care of these vehicles. We should be able to find what is needed there. I think three will be needed. Red knows what to look for and one of your men and myself.

That should be enough." Suddenly there was some commotion. One of the men standing watch, spotted a vehicle coming through the forest toward their location traveling on the dirt road. We turned to see what he saw.

"Well, it looks like we found a way to get to the camp. Red, stand close to those trees, over there I think, let them see you. But don't do anything that will start them shooting."

"What? Do what?

"Hurry, get over there, we need that jeep there driving. That's going to be our transportation."

"Captain, if you don't mind I need to borrow one man."

The Captain nodded and gesture to Yatt to do what Gray asked of them...

"What is your name? Gray asked

"Yett is my name."

"Yatt, when that jeep gets up here I need you to take out the two men. Don't kill them and don't get killed. The weapons they have shoots an object that can kill you I think."

He nodded and went around to the other side of rock that gave him cover. The Jeep was coming at full speed now that they saw Red near the tree line. Red was doing some kind of acting, to keep their attention, but not enough to have them fire at him. You could hear them yelling at Red to stay where he is and not move. Their weapon were drawn and pointing directly at Red.

As the jeep came around the side of the rock it stopped and the two men jumped out yelling and giving orders. They pointed there weapons, waving them around. Red waved his hands above his head," Don't Shoot", don't shoot," he continually shouted back. "Don't shoot, I give up."

Within seconds Yatt appeared from behind the rock and with the speed of a cat he darted at the back of both men and with several blows, both were laying on the ground.

"Wow," Red commented as he went over to Yatt and help drag the men into the trees. He reached into the jeep a found some rope and tied the two to a tree. He checked their pockets and found nothing other than half of a cigar.

Yatt and Red came back together. Yatt walked proudly. He single handedly took out two men. The others gathered around him. Probably praising him. Asking him how it felt.

"This jeep will get us into the camp area faster and get us back even quicker." Gray stated standing by the jeep. "We'll leave as soon as it's at its darkest."

"How was my performance? Red asked

"Stellar, Red, just stellar. Captain Kirk would be proud of you. In fact it reminded me of something I saw once in a move."

"Really, I was that convincing. I was afraid they were going to start shooting."

"They wanted you alive, they needed to bring you back to find out who you are, what you're doing on their island." Gray replied.

"But your performance was excellent and kept their attention on you so they could be taken out."

"I think this should be part of our training." Red replied.

"Well, you're going to have to convince someone that this situation warrants a new chapter in Naval Pilot Survival Training."

"Diversionary tactics. We'll call it." Red said. "I need to write this down. You got a pencil or pen?

CHAPTER SIX

After waiting another hour, it was dark enough for them to leave. They needed to be able to slip into the compound quietly and gather what was needed and get back without being seen. This would give them enough time to make the repairs. Any conflict that could occur needed to be handled quickly and just as quietly.

Red brought the jeep over to where the others were standing. "If we're going to do this, we need to go now. "Why don't we use the hose from the jeep? Red asked.

"Because if we run into problems, we'll need the jeep to lead them away from here. Besides there other reasons as well." Gray replied.

"How are going to explain all this when we get rescued? Have you thought about that at all? This is not an easy topic to discuss. Even believe." Red commented while they waited for Yatt to appear.

"We'll worry about that when the time comes, and I hope this works, I'd like there to be another time."

Yatt finally came out. He walked toward the jeep carrying several different objects and an outfit that must be their version of battle wear. It made him look twice the size with all the attachments and padding or armor that was on his suit."

"This guy really looks like something out of the science fiction movies. What is all that stuff? Red asked.

"I have no idea. He must weigh close to 350 to 400 pounds if not more. He surely won't fit in the jeep. See if he can fit in the back, if he hangs his legs over the side."

Red jumped out of the jeep and went to the back and waited for Yatt. He tried to explain how he needs to sit, to be able to fit into the jeep. Yatt climbed into the back of the jeep, hung his feet over the side. Just then the rear of the jeep sank down.

"Are the front wheels even touching the ground? Gray asked.

Red looked before getting behind the wheel. He nodded and started the jeep. It creaked as it moved through the dirt road. The others stood watching as the jeep drove away. They appeared to be pointing at the jeep and laughing at what they saw. Yatt's feet were dragging on the ground as the jeep moved.

There were so many pot holes in the road that Red had to swerve around them. Red hit one pot hole hard enough that Yatt bounced out of the jeep and landed on the road. Red stopped the jeep and looked back to see Yatt sitting on the ground. They watched as Yatt got up, started dusting himself off, walked back to the jeep and then climbed back into seat. The others laughed.

They reached the outer area of the camp and pulled off the road into the growth of trees. Red turned the jeep around positioning it for a fast retreat. They walked the balance of the way until the camp was totally visible and slowly hid themselves behind a large stack of drums. The camps grounds were dimly lit and several vehicles were parked near a large building.

"Stay here, I want to see what we're dealing with." Gray whispered.

He moved through the stack of barrels, watching for any guards that might be positioned. He reached the back side of a truck. The building in front of the truck was a wooden structure with a front door that was left open with crates stacked against it. There were several other building and many open face coverings further down the line from this building. He could see lights on in the distance in buildings that must house the workers. As he remained hidden he suddenly heard a thud from behind him. A body of a man hit the ground and an assault rifle laid next to him.

Gray turned around quickly to see Yatt standing behind him with Red next to him. Red nodded and smiled.

"Thought you could use some help."

"Where did he come from? Gray asked quietly with a surprised look on his face.

Red pointed to a place next to the building near the back. Gray took a deep breath, then looked up at Yatt. Yatt nodded, then patted Red on the back. Red just smiled.

"We need to get inside this building. I think this is their maintenance building for the trucks. The parts we need could be inside. Yatt and I will stay out here and keep watch. You see if you can find what you need, and don't take all day doing it. There must be other guards around somewhere." Gray explained.

Red slowly moved around the truck and into the building while Gray and Yatt stationed themselves in positions that allowed them to view the camp grounds, especially the buildings that appeared to be barracks. At times they could hear the sound of laughter, arguing and shouting.

Red moved slowly inside the building. The inside was cluttered with crates, boxes and odd parts. Along the outer wall was a long counter. Parts were scattered along the counter top. Red moved carefully, trying to avoid the items that lay on the ground. Knocking anything over could cause a problem and bring the entire camp down on them. The darkness of the building limited Red ability to see clearly. The windows had no glass in them and allow some night light to enter.

When he reached the end of the counter he found what he was looking for. A new radiator hose that was about the right diameter. He moved some of the junk that was stacked on the counter looking for some clamps. There above a box filled with different sized nails were several clamps. Grabbing the clamps he placed them in his pocket and looked around for any containers of radiator fluid. He needed at least five gallons of radiator fluid to fill the cooling reservoir. He continued searching, going from box to box, moving items around, and then finally stopped. Nothing that he could see.

"There must be some here somewhere. If I only had some light so I could see." He said in a shallow voice.

As he moved back toward the door he bumped into a large cardboard box. Written on the side in large black letters was the word orange juice. Red thought for a minute and opened the lid. He picked up a package of powered concentrated orange juice. He put several into the pocket of his pants. When he turned to see what else was around. There stacked against the wall where several containers of radiator fluid. He hurried over and took as many as he could carry and took them outside. He stopped suddenly and set them down.

"What's this? Red softly said looking at several more bodies lying on the ground.

"While you were in there, we were busy out here. I hope you found what we needed because this is getting a little crowded out here. I think Yatt is enjoying this," Lt. Gray replied as he stepped over one of the bodies, picking up one of the containers that Red brought out.

"This is a familiar brand."

"We need a total of six of these containers. Here's four. I'll get the rest, then let's get out of here."

Red hurried back inside and brought out two more containers and they started to leave, back through the stacked barrels. They moved quickly making sure they were not seen. They reached the edge of the forest and made their way to the hidden jeep. They quickly stacked the containers in the back leaving enough room for Yatt to get his large body in.

The jeep moved, creaked and felt sluggish with the weight of Yatt and all the other items and bodies. Red kept the lights off which made it difficult to see and avoid many of the large ruts in the road. Everyone bounced around until they were far enough away. Red turned the lights on and they sped away at a faster speed.

"They're going to find those bodies soon. We need to get the repairs done quickly and get them out of here before they find us. When it's first light I'll need to contact the Enterprise."

"What are you going to tell them," Red asked as he maneuvered the jeep along the dirt road.

"I don't know." He replied. "I'll think of something when the times comes. Our main concern will be getting there ship repaired.

They returned and unloaded the coolant. Making his way to the ship, Yatt carried the coolant inside with Red following behind him.

"Lt. Gray I see that you found what was needed." He asked. "Did you have any problems?

"We had a few issues that occurred, but Yatt took care of it. He is very efficient in what he does."

"Yes, he is one of our very best. He is very dedicated and is a loyal soldier. He has been with me for a long time. We have encounter many situations together."

"Red says that he should have everything finished within thirty minutes. You'll be able leave soon. We were interrupted several times and had to make a few minor adjustments while we were there." Gray explained. "They'll probably find our adjustments when it comes light, and they will probably come looking for us."

"As I have heard through your language a saying that says, ***there is a need for speed***."

"Yes Sir, you are right about that. We should be able to see them coming. If you can make sure one of your men is stationed above those rocks." Gray asked pointing to the area.

Captain Org gave the order. Quickly one man hurried and climbed the large boulder to the top.

"Now, let's hope Red was right and all they needed was the hose and clamps. I don't think we'll have a second chance to go back into the camp for more parts."

Org nodded. "I understand. You risked your life for us. You are a good soldier Lt. Gray. Your world must be proud of you and your companion."

"Well, let's say Captain, there is a lot at stake here.

Chapter Seven

Red returned from the ship, as the others completed the repairs. He was fixing himself a cup of orange drink from the packets he had found in the building.

"Where did you get that? Gray asked.

"Found a case of it in the building when I was looking for the coolant. I forgot I had it, want some?

"No that's okay. Are they almost finished?

"We had to flush out the tank before putting in the coolant. I didn't think it was a good idea to mix ours with there's. The hose is connected and the clamps fit perfectly. There putting everything back together. Shouldn't take no more than ten minutes."

"Good, it's going to be light pretty soon, and I think the funs about to get started."

"Where did you get that cup from? Gray asked.

"It's a fold up cup from our survival items, you got one." Red explained.

Lt. Gray walked over to where Captain Org stood. He could see that he was still concerned.

"Being stranded on a planet, I can't imagine what that must be like." Gray stated.

Captain Org, staring off into the sky line, turned and sat down on a rock. "Being a soldiers of outer space can have its issues no matter where you end up. I have been doing this for a long time. My travels have taken me many places. It is always something that I must consider. My worry is for my crew. They are young, except for Yatt. They have not experienced the many situations that come with this type of military duty."

"Are they married? Do they have families? Gray asked.

"We are no different than you. We look different, because our planet is different. But we are basically the same. I have a family. All of these soldiers have families. We have a structure which limits the size of our families. Our government is controlled by a body of elected high ranking military leaders. We have homes and transportation vehicles like you have. Our technology, as you can imagine, is far advanced than yours and has been for hundreds of years."

"Have you fought many battles? Gray asked.

"Very few of our battles involve soldiers. We do not destroy a world as your planet has in the past. Our wars have allow the planet to eliminate the life source, without destroying the planets elements."

"I was going to ask the magic question, if there are others like you. Other civilizations that exist? Gray asked. "You answered that question."

"Yes, there are many. Many that are be-on your ability to reach. Not all are friendly as you are, but they live in their own developed world."

Red walked over and sat down.

"I just gave Yatt some of this orange drink. He saw me drinking it and wanted to try it."

"Yatt," yelled Captain Org. Yatt heard the call and walked over and joined them. He spoke in their language which appeared to be more of an order of some kind.

"I told him not to indulge himself. Your form of food and drink is not the same as ours. Our bodies have a different chemical makeup."

Just then a loud sound occurred along with a terrible smell. Captain Org yelled at Yatt, and Yatt quickly hurried away. "This is why we never indulge ourselves of fluids or foods from other planets."

The smell over took us and we all scattered in different directions. We could hear him from where we were, still having the same reaction to the orange drink. The other soldiers around him were shouting at him as well and they too scattered.

"Well, I guess he's not going to get any more of this." Red said. "I never thought that would happen."

"They should be done soon. The metal covering are heavy and they have to fit just so. I sure hope the coolant we used will provide them what they need."

"I think all they need is to get into orbit. They have a support ship on its way. He said it was two days out, now one day. The sun will be up real soon. If they find the bodies we left behind, you can bet as soon as there is light, they'll be looking for us and things will get very dicey.

"We've never been a part of anything even remotely like this. What a story it's going to make when we get back." Red stated. "Having been stranded on an island with aliens from another world. Wait till Edington hears this. He may lock us both up. You don't think he'll toss us over the side will he?

"There's always that chance. You can swim can't you?

"I fly better than I can swim"

"Listen Red, I don't want you to do anything that will get you shot. If things get out of control, stay out of the way of the action. These are not military soldiers under the command of a military leader. These are men who take orders from a corrupt leader who probably is more concerned for himself and his goods. He'd shoot his own men if placed in the wrong conditions. So be careful."

"I don't intend on getting myself shot. I have too much to do." Red replied.

CHAPTER EIGHT

The sun came up and the heat of the sun warmed the air. It felt good. The early morning sky was a soft blue with not a cloud anywhere. Captain Org. had several of his men stationed in different positions watching the landscape for intruders. The craft was operating and they were preparing it to lift off. Suddenly one of the men shouted something and we all turned to look. From a distance we could he the sound of vehicles moving through the depth of the forest. Captain Org ran over to see.

"This is it Captain, you need to leave now, right now. Get your men aboard. Red and I will take the jeep and lead them off into the forest. When you see the last vehicle pass by and they enter into the forest after us, leave." Gray explained as he ran over to the jeep. He called for Red."

"Lt. Gray, you are giving up yourself so that we may escape. You are sacrificing your lives." Org replied.

"There's no time for discussion Captain, get aboard your ship and be ready to go."

"Red jumped into the jeep. "I'd like to discuss this."

"Later." Gray replied.

Gray turned the jeep around and placed in sight. As soon as he was able to see the lead vehicle he followed the dirt road into the forest at a slow speed. Making sure that he was visible to the enemy convoy that was coming. Red turned around to see how far behind them they were. He suddenly heard a popping sound coming from the distance.

"I think there shooting at us." He said with a concerned tone.

"You think so," Gray replied. "Have they cleared the area yet?

Suddenly a bright light lit up the sky and a long trail of light streaked across the horizon then disappeared into the darkness of space.

"They just did." Red replied.

"How close are they to us now? Gray asked.

"Close enough to throw a rock at us." Red said as he hung on to the side of the jeep as it hit another pot hole in the road.

"I can't go every fast, these ruts in the road slow us down."

Red could hear the sound of bullets whizzing by. He continued to duck and crouch down in the jeep.

"Their getting closer with their aim." Red said as he heard the sound of a bullet hitting the back of the jeep.

"They're not going to shoot us. They want us alive. We're more important to them alive than died."

"And you know this how? Red asked as he got lower in the seat.

Suddenly there was a large explosion next to the jeep. Dirt and debris covered the jeep, but Gray continued to drive.

"That was too close." He shouted. "They got one of those hand held rocket launchers. Can you see it?

Again another blast from further ahead of them tore into the ground causing Gray to swivel to the right to avoid the hole from the blast.

"This is getting a little intense." Gray shouted.

Red, who continued to remain crouched in the seat, raised up slightly. "Intense is not the word I would use."

"Ahead of us is a thicker layer of trees. If we can get inside there before they blow us to pieces we might be able to get away. Are they getting to close?

"There close enough, here comes another incoming." Red yelled out, then ducked down into the seat.

The blast was close enough to force the jeep to swerve to the right and then flip over on its side. It skidded on its side until it hit a large boulder and stopped.

"Red, are you alright? Gray asked.

"Yeah, I'm okay." He replied back as he lifted himself up from the ground. The jeep tossed me out. You okay, any injuries?

Gray was also thrown from the jeep when it flipped on its side He quickly got up. He ran over to Red and grabbed him by the arm.

"Let's go, we need to get out of here."

They tried to run into the thickness of the forest, but could not out run the vehicles. Several shots were fired and a whole lot of yelling was going on as Lt Gray and Red tried to elude them. They made several quick turns, ducked in behind some rocks, and then made several moves to change directions.

Onboard the Enterprise, Edington had just completed another call. But no reply. He continually requested that he be allowed to send in some type of support but was told that any attempt would need authorization from higher up and he must wait.

"Captain Edington, we've had no contact with Gray Goose since last night. His next communication is well overdue."

"Okay, I'll be in the Situation Room. If you get any information at all, let me know."

Edington left and hurried to the Situation Room. He punched in his code and the door opened slowly. Two armed Marines stood on each side of the outer door.

"Okay, let's get this screen going. I want to see what's going on"

"Yes Sir, We'll have satellite hookup in ten seconds. The Island is going to be difficult because of the many rock formation. But if there in the open we should be able to see what going on."

"Here we go Sir, We are online now. Let me bring their forms in closer." The operator said as the screen began coming into vision.

"What are we looking at?

"The forms that you see is Lt. Gray and Red moving, no their running. Something is after them. See the forms to the right of the screen. There appears to be ten, no twelve individuals chasing after them."

Everyone in the situation room watched closely as the event unfolded on the screen. Gray and Red were desperately trying to out maneuver the enemy but there were too many and the landscape was difficult to maneuver through.

"It will just a matter of minutes before they are over taken Sir. There closing in on them now."

Within a few minutes Gray and Red were over taken and now in the hands of the bandits of the island. Everyone watched the green screen. Some with sadness, others angry that nothing was done.

"Sir, we can't just sit here and watch our men become prisoners. They are not a military force of another country, why can't we just send in a team in and get the Gray Goose and Red out of there?

"I know what you want. We don't make policy we carry it out. I want them back just as much as you do. But until we get the go ahead, we'll just have to watch and hope that nothing happens to them. Once we get the go ahead I'll send in the entire ship's crew if I have to. But until we get the okay, we'll have to just watch."

"Sir, it appears that they're being taken to the camp. It looks like it's the building at the far end of the grounds."

"Keep your attention on them. If there is any change in their position, let me know. I'm going to call again and see if I can get things moving a little faster." Edington stated.

Chapter Nine

Lt. Gray and Red were placed on the ground next to the jeep. Three men tied their hands behind their backs and helped get them to their feet. A man, who appeared to be in charge walked over to them. He was a heavy man, thick with abundant black hair and a thick beard. An AK 47 was hanging on his back. His shirt was half way unbutton and heavy sweat stains cover his shirt.

"Well…seniors, what have we got here, two spies. You are Americans soldiers, pilot no doubt. I am Pedro Mendoza and you've evaded our great paradise, seniors. The American government was ordered to stay away from this place. What are you doing here? He asked as he walked back in fourth in front of them. Never mind, we will talk later. Put them in the back of the truck and lets us go." He said with a heavy accent. The men guarding them pushed them toward the truck. The Leader shouted something and several men went over to the jeep and began to lift the jeep back onto its wheels.

The truck traveled on the dirt road, through the forest, and into the camp. Inside the canopy of the truck, Gray could look out the back and see the buildings pass by and other vehicles. The truck stopped and the two guards inside jumped down while two other men removed the tail gate. The one men shouted at Gray and Red to jump down from the truck, then led them into an old rusted tin building.

They walked past several tables that were being used to prepare drugs for shipment. Packages and packages, all neatly secured and bundled where stacked on the table. As they walked to the rear of the building they could see the boxes of neatly stacked bundles of money. Stacks and Stacks of cash. When they reached the end of the building they were each tied to the wall. Their hands above their head.

"Well Seniors, this is your new home." The one said as he laughed and walked away. The others laughed as well. Two men stayed behind to guard them. They sat on two chairs and lit up two cigars, blowing out large clouds of smoke. The placed their rifles against the aluminum wall.

"Red, we're sure in a pickle now. If I know Edington he be following us using the satellite imaging system from the Situation Room. They should nowhere we're at."

"I sure hope so." Red replied back. "I sure hope so."

Edington began to pace back and forth. "Can we see into that building? Edington asked.

"No Sir, only because the satellite system has passed over and is now on a new position out of our reach. I need to wait a few minutes so that we can connect to another that will be passing over in about five minutes."

"How many do we have up there? Edington asked.

"Well Sir, it's pretty crowded up there. Not just ours but the Soviet Union. They have a few of their own. We can use there's if you want me to patch into them. I'm sure the Russians after a while will figure out why were using there satellites."

"No, I don't need more problems right now. If we have one coming over, we'll use it. Let's keep the Russians out of our business."

"Sir, with all the junk flying around up there I'm sure someone already knows that something is going on."

Within a few minutes the Enterprise was connected with a new satellite link and were focused on what was going on. They knew the position of Gray and Red and were now able keep track of their where location. Several hours had passed and still no communication concerning any type of rescue.

Inside the building, Mendoza and several of his men walked to several areas of the building. They inspected the work that was going on and made sure everything was functioning correctly. He would yell at several of his workers and argue with others on what they were doing. He knew what he wanted done and expected them to follow through with his demands. He appeared to be a very demanding leader with no patience for mistakes. Mendoza argued with one man. He began yelling and shouting, then he slapped him. The older man fell to the ground. Two men grabbed the man and drug him out of the building. When he reached the back of the building he walked over to where Gray and Red with located. They began talking to one another laughing.

"I see you are still with us seniors. You must favor our fine establishment. Now you can tell me why you are on my island? What is it you want?

Gray and Red said nothing. They remain silent.

"Come now seniors, I've been good to you. You are not hurt or injured. You can at least tell me what your plans are before we shoot you. I don't want to be unhospitable but I've got no time for you. I've have much business to attend to."

Gray and Red still remained silent. His words had a quick effect on Red.

"I was thinking, you are a pilot senior. You must have flown in here or something. But we have not seen anything of that nature. We are further from your land. You must have come from a very large ship. Is there a, what you call a flat top, out from our shores. Your fighter jets cannot come this far without the need of refueling?

Gray and Red still stayed silent. At times they would stare directly at Mendoza when he spoke and other times they would look away. Their training was very clear on what procedures to follow when one becomes a prisoner of war. They were not at war but they were certainly prisoners.

"Look Seniors, You have seen what we have. You must know that I cannot let you go, so why don't you use your head and tell me what I ask. Maybe I'll let you live a little longer, maybe have a last meal. Smoke a good cigar."

Gray finally spoke. "My name is Lt. Daniel L. Gray, USS Naval Pilot, number 554789891."

"He can speak after all." Mendoza said. "But I don't care who you are, but why you are here Senior. You with the funny red hair, do you speak?

'My name is Herman C. Hansen. US Naval Engineer first class. The best in the business. Number 667694567."

Mendoza looked at the others who were standing by. Many of them began to laugh. "You are called Red. You must have that name because of your red hair." The others laughed.

Mendoza turned, "Pedro, shoot this little man with the red hair. Then through him into the sea for the fishes."

Pedro smiled took the cigar out of his mouth and walked over to where

AK47 is was sitting, picked it up and check it. He was a beer belly of a man. His belly laid over his belt. He had sweat stains on his shirt and tears in his pants and sloppy. He walked over to Red, and pointed the barrel at Red head, then he smiled and laughed, showing most of his missing front teeth.

"Senior, you ready to meet your maker? Pedro said as he placed the barrel of the rifle against Red's head. "Maybe you got something you want to say, or you want to pray, or maybe you just want it over with. Which one you want Senior? Red took a deep breathe. Sweat was rolling down the side of his face.

Suddenly there was shouting and gun fire. Men were running in and out of the building. Mendoza quickly hurried over to the doorway. "What's happening," he asked as one of his men came running by. The man just kept on running, not answering.

Mendoza grabbed another man as he came by and through him against the outer wall. "What's going on, who are you running from, who are they shooting at?

"Monsters, monsters." The man replied. "Lots of them." He pushed Mendoza away and ran off screaming to others.

"Monsters, what is he talking about, Monsters? Mendoza replied. He turned to his men and shouted at them. "Go, see what that crazy man was talking about, go on."

Suddenly, all of the men were running by. Some stopped to fire their weapons. Other dropped their weapons to the ground and just ran off into the forest, yelling and shouting. Mendoza turned to see what was creating all the pandemonium. His eyes opened wide and saw an invasion of things charging toward him. They fired their weapons and everything they hit disappeared into flames. They came closer and began tearing the buildings apart. Many were on fire and burning.

"What are they? He shouted out. "What are they? He dropped his weapon and began running along with the others into the forest. Pushing and shoving others out of the way so he could escape.

"What's going on out there? Gray asked. "Who's doing all the shooting?"

"Maybe it's a task group from the Enterprise." Red replied.

"Maybe, but I don't think so. We wouldn't be sitting everything on fire. The whole place is burning."

Edington watched as the invasion took place. "What is going on," He said with a surprised look. "Who are they?" He asked again as he saw a large group come out from nowhere and began the assault on the camp.

"Sir, I'm not sure who this group is, but we have located a large heat source which normally only comes from a powerful jet engine.

"So this group who is attacking the camp got there from a something that we can't see."

"Basically, yes."

There was noise from the front of the building as Captain Org came walking into the building. He was carrying a weapon and wearing some kind of armor suit. He was followed by six or seven other soldiers who rushed in. He saw where Gray and Red were at and ordered his men to untie us.

"Lt. Gray," he said. "I hope you and Red are alright and not injured. We were able to meet up with our support group. I could not let you sacrifice yourself for us. We made our presents known. But we needed to secure your safety. Most of them have run into the forest and will probably keep running for some time. Shall we leave this place and return you to your vessel."

As we prepared to leave, Captain Org walked through the building and noticed the bundles inside the boxes.

"What are these? He asked as he looked at the bundles of money neatly stacked inside the boxes.

"That is money from those who purchased the drugs."

"You use this to purchase things? He asked

"Yes."

He ordered his soldiers to take the boxes and place them in his craft. Gray and Red watched as soldiers carried the boxes across the camp grounds and loaded them into his craft.

"What's he doing? Red asked.

"I'm not sure, but I'm not going to interfere with his plans."

After all of the soldiers were accounted for and the returned to their ships. Captain Org waved to us to come aboard. Red, excited about the invitation, hurried to the ship. We were given seats in the rear, and provided with masks that would allow us to breathe our air. Yatt sat in front with Captain Org as the ship powered up. The interior was an incredible sight of electronics, lights and buttons. You could feel the power of the engineers as the ship lifted off from the ground. It began to move, and move quickly as it skimmed across the sky at a speed that was be on anything one could imagine.

"This ship is an engineer's dream. It has components that do things we never thought of." Red said.

"Where are we going," Red asked

Captain Org seat began to move. You could hear a motor engage as the seat slowly turned. "We are going to take you to your ship."

"Won't that cause a problem? Red asked.

"I think they are probably knowing that there is something going on that is unexplainable. Lt. I want you to do the talking for us to your leadership."

"I need to contact them and tell them we're coming. What they don't understand my cause them to think they are being attacked or at least endanger."

"I agree. Yatt will prepare the transmission for you. You will be able to speak to your commanding officer."

Gray got on the radio. It was designed much like all radios but just looked slightly different. Radio transmissions are basic. Yatt was able to find the correct frequency. Yatt nodded.

"Enterprise, this is Gray Goose. Come in."

"Captain Edington, we have communication from Gray Goose." Edington hurried over to the radio.

"Gray Goose this is Enterprise, We are receiving your transmission. What is you location."

"Enterprise, we need the deck cleared for landing."

"Gray Goose, please repeat, landing where? He asked.

"Enterprise we have a sensitive need that requires your assistance. Please clear the deck. Have everyone report to their quarters. No one must be on deck. There can be no eyes."

Edington had no idea what was happening. But if it brings the two back on board he'll do it. "Have the deck cleared and have everyone report to the quarters." It was announced according to Edington's orders. The deck was cleared and Edington ordered the speed reduced, then all stop.

"Gray Goose your request has been approved and the deck is now cleared for landing. Do you require any additional help on the deck?

"Enterprise this is Gray Goose, No additional help is needed. Please tell Captain Edington to be prepared for officials."

"What's he talking about," Edington replied. "What officials? He turned to Lt. Turner. Alright, all stop.

"Aye, Captain, all stop.

"Sir, I have a group of what appears to be some type of air craft approaching from the West. There is a total of seven."

"What kind of air craft? He asked

"I'm not able to identify its type, other than it is now visible. One is about to land on the deck. It's waiting for the ship to come to a stop."

Edington walked out and was followed by several other ranking officers. They reached the flight deck door and opened it. What they saw stopped them.

"What is that?

Edington said nothing but stood staring at what had just landed on his carrier. It was nothing that he had ever seen before in all his years as a naval officer and pilot.

"Now I know why Gray wanted the deck cleared." Edington said as he took another step forward then turned around. "Make sure all personal are in there quarters, now." He demanded.

The craft landed softly on the deck. It was large, covering half of the width of the carrier's deck. It stood seven to eight feet above the deck surface standing on three landing legs. It had a v-shaped design with wings that extended out from its side and no tail wings. There were windows only in the front and were darkened. Heat came off the craft. A lower door open under the craft. A smell of a gases odor came from the opening as the door reached the carriers surface. Several seconds passed. Edington and his officers watched with amazement at what was occurring. Finally Gray and Red came out from under the craft. They walked over to Captain Edington, stood at attention and saluted. Edington saluted back still not saying a word.

"Lt. Gray and Engineer First Class Red."

"Lt.... Red, we are glad that the both of you are well and have returned to us in one piece." Edington replied. "I'm not sure what I'm looking at, so

I hope that you can explain what's happening, so I can make some sense of this."

"Yes Sir." Gray replied back. "I would like to introduce to you Captain Org and his First Officer Yatt."

Edington watched as the two walked toward them. His eyes widened as he saw two being walking to them. He was speechless at first and said nothing.

"I know Captain that you are probably stunned at our sight. May I offer you my hand in friendship? Lt. Gray has explained that is your custom in greeting someone." Org. said has he held out his hand.

Edington looked at Org's large hand. He wore some type of glove. He reached out and shook Org's hand. He was big, almost seven foot tall. His decals on his uniform indicated he was a higher ranking officer than his first officer, who was as tall but much heavier.

"Captain Org, The United States Navy welcomes you aboard the USS Enterprise."

Yet appeared to get excited when he heard the name Enterprise, and was continually looking around at the sights. "We had to make a very delicate decision Captain Edington. To expose ourselves openly to you. Our experience with your kind, especially Lt. Gray and engineer Red has softened our thoughts. We want you to know as their commanding officer. These two men were willing to sacrifice themselves so that we could escape and therefore not be discovered. We like your kind, honor bravery and courage and could not allow these two soldiers to be captured and possibly killed. We have returned them to you unharmed.

"Captain Org. The United State Navy thanks you for what must have been a very difficult decision to make and returning our men to us."

"I have two additional requests to ask of you."

"Certainly, Captain." Edington replied.

"I ask that our existence be our secret. And that you instruct your men not to speak of us. I do not believe that our two worlds are ready to meet. There is much to learn still. Maybe in the future when our worlds have settled down, we will be able to meet."

"I will ensure you that we will take all precautions and instruct our personal in your request."

"Lastly, we are responsible for the destruction of Lt. Gray's air craft.

We would like to replace it using this to purchase a new one. I understand that this is used for such things."

Everyone watched as the soldiers delivered the boxes of cash that was taken from the island. They stacked the boxes in front of Edington. Everyone was stunned by the quantity of cash that was in front of them.

"I hope this enough to purchase a new one." Captain Org said as the last box was delivered and stacked.

"I'm sure that will do Captain Org." Edington replied. He turned and ordered his officers to gather the boxes and take them inside and place them in a secured location.

"We must now leave. My support craft are just off shore waiting for our return. We say our good byes now. Captain Edington saluted and shook Org's hand. Org turned to Lt. Gray and saluted him.

"My world and my people thank you. If you ever need any help of any kind please feel free to contact me."

Org placed a small device into Lt. Gray's hand. "This will provide direct contact to me or Yatt."

"I will." Gray replied, placing the object into the pocket of his flight suit. He watched as the Org and Yatt started to leave and return to their space craft. Red had left and returned. He ran over to Yatt carrying a small box.

"Yatt, here I want you to have this." Red yelled out. "This is the series from Star Trek. You'll have to learn to read our language, but I know you have the technology to do it. I put a little something in there for you as well."

Yatt smiled, reached up and ran his big hand through Red's red hair and took the box. Captain Org and Yatt walked to the opening of the ship climbed up the latter as the door began to close behind them.

"What did you give him? Gray asked.

The engines began to roar and then began to hum. Suddenly the door opened again and a packet of orange drink was tossed out of the craft, landing on the deck.

"You gave him some of the orange drink that was in our flight suits? Gray asked with a smile on his face.

"He liked it."

The space crafts lifted off the Enterprises deck and quickly rose to a height and then accelerated quickly. The powerful engines pushed the craft through the air without any effort. From a distance another group of space craft passed by in formation. Soon all had vanished from view.

Red and Gray sat with Captain Edington and provided all the details of the events that took place. There was much to discuss and how to explain what had happened to the naval brass and Washington was going to be even more of a problem.

"Well, I've got at least a day or two to think about what to say. We should be in port by Sunday afternoon." Edington remarked. "The two of you need to keep this silent, and to yourself. What we have seen today will have to be dealt with in the near future. But at least we have had some advanced contact and have some understand between the two worlds. I need a drink."

"I guess this answers the question, are we alone" Gray states as he and Red leave together.

"You know, when I first saw them I didn't know what to think or say. I was speechless. All I saw was something that was probably too unbelievable, horrifying at first. My heart was about to jump out of my chest. The unknown can be a dangerous thing. We or even they could have made the wrong decision. That could have been a disaster. What an experience we had."

"Yeah, and make sure you keep it to yourself." Gray stated as the two began to walk away.

"I'm not good at keeping secrets," Red replied.

"You will with this one or over the side you'll go."

THE END

OR IS IT?

The USS Enterprise is a US Navy aircraft carrier. It was the first nuclear powered aircraft carrier in the World and the eight United States Naval vessel to bear that name, with the nickname of "The Big E." It was also the longest and the oldest active combat vessel in the Navy.

www.enterprise.navy.mil

Printed in the United States
By Bookmasters